Peppa Pig

Peppa's Circus

Peppa and her friends are visiting
Granny and Grandpa Pig.

"What's that?" asks Pedro Pony.
"Is it the circus?" wonders
Suzy Sheep.
"No," says Grandpa Pig.
"It is a tent for
Granny Pig's garden party."

The children decide to make their own circus.
"We can call it Peppa's Circus!" says Peppa.

Granny Pig thinks this is a splendid idea.
She fetches the dressing-up box.

There are lots of good circus costumes
in the dressing-up box.

Peppa finds a top hat. Danny Dog finds some spotty trunks and a stick-on moustache.

The garden party guests arrive.
Granny Pig shows them into
the tent.

"Ladies and gentlemen," cries Peppa.
"Welcome to my circus!"

"Now," says Peppa. "Please be very scared of the amazing Candy Cat!"
Rebecca Rabbit holds out a hoop for Candy Cat to jump through.

Growl!

Squeak!

George, Richard and
Edmond come out next.

Creak!

They ride round and
round on their tricycles.

"Don't stop clapping,"
calls Peppa. "Here's the strong Danny Dog!"

Danny lifts Peppa high up into the air.

The crowd goes wild. Danny Dog is very strong.

Now it is Emily Elephant's turn. She juggles two potatoes and an egg.

"Oooooh!" gasps the audience.

It is the end of Peppa's
amazing circus.
"That," Granny Pig laughs, "is
the best circus I have ever seen!"